This Book Belongs To:

....

Illustrated by Victoria Assanelli

This edition published by Parragon Books Ltd in 2014
Parragon Books Ltd
Chartist House
15-17 Trim Street
Bath BA1 1HA, UK
www.parragon.com

ISBN 978-1-4723-7418-9

Printed in China

The Twelve Days of Christmas

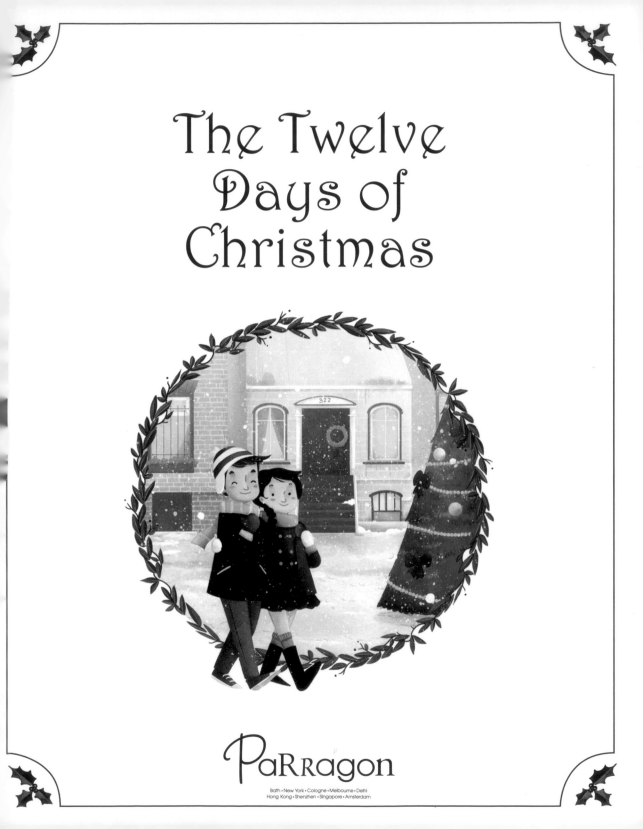

Parragon

Bath · New York · Cologne · Melbourne · Delhi
Hong Kong · Shenzhen · Singapore · Amsterdam

On the first day of Christmas
my true love sent to me
A partridge in a pear tree.

On the second day of Christmas
my true love sent to me
Two turtle doves

And a partridge in a pear tree.

On the third day of Christmas
    my true love sent to me
Three French hens,

Two turtle doves
And a partridge in a pear tree.

On the fourth day of Christmas
my true love sent to me
Four calling birds,

Three French hens,
Two turtle doves
And a partridge in a pear tree.

On the fifth day of Christmas
my true love sent to me

Five golden rings...

Four calling birds,
Three French hens,
Two turtle doves
And a partridge in a pear tree.

On the sixth day of Christmas
my true love sent to me
Six geese a laying,

Five golden rings,
Four calling birds,
Three French hens,
Two turtle doves
And a partridge in a pear tree.

On the seventh day of Christmas
my true love sent to me
Seven swans a-swimming,

Six geese a-laying,
Five golden rings,
Four calling birds,
Three French hens,
Two turtle doves
And a partridge in a pear tree.

On the eighth day of Christmas
my true love sent to me
Eight maids a-milking,

Seven swans a-swimming,
Six geese a-laying,
Five golden rings,
Four calling birds,
Three French hens,
Two turtle doves
And a partridge in a pear tree.

On the ninth day of Christmas
my true love sent to me
Nine ladies dancing,

Eight maids a-milking,
Seven swans a-swimming,
Six geese a-laying,
Five golden rings,
Four calling birds,
Three French hens,
Two turtle doves
And a partridge in a pear tree.

On the tenth day of Christmas
my true love sent to me
Ten lords a-leaping,

Nine ladies dancing,
Eight maids a-milking,
Seven swans a-swimming,
Six geese a-laying,
Five golden rings,
Four calling birds,
Three French hens,
Two turtle doves
And a partridge in a pear tree.

On the eleventh day of Christmas
my true love sent to me
Eleven pipers piping,

Ten lords a-leaping,
Nine ladies dancing,
Eight maids a-milking,
Seven swans a-swimming,
Six geese a-laying,
Five golden rings,
Four calling birds,
Three French hens,
Two turtle doves
And a partridge in a pear tree.

On the twelfth day of Christmas
my true love sent to me
Twelve drummers drumming,

Eleven pipers piping,
Ten lords a-leaping,
Nine ladies dancing,
Eight maids a-milking,
Seven swans a-swimming,
Six geese a-laying,
Five golden rings,
Four calling birds,
Three French hens,
Two turtle doves
And a partridge in a pear tree!